BITTEN BY AN IRRADIATED SPIDER, WHICH GRANTED HIM INCREDIBLE ABILITIES, **PETER PARKER** LEARNED THE ALL-IMPORTANT LESSON, THAT WITH GREAT POWER THERE MUST ALSO COME GREAT RESPONSIBILITY. AND SO HE BECAME THE AMAZING SPIDER-MAN

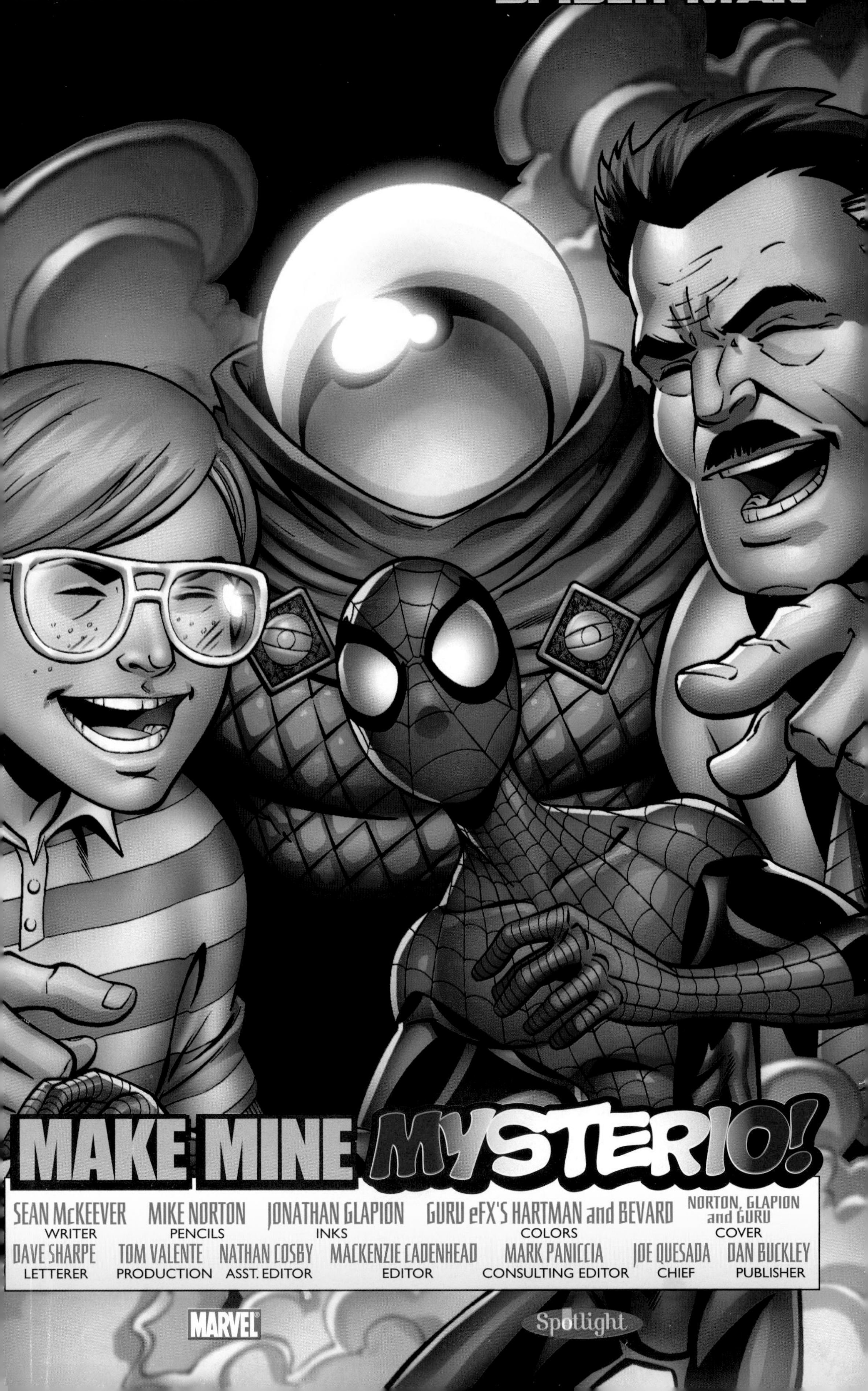

MAKE MINE MYSTERIO!

SEAN McKEEVER WRITER
MIKE NORTON PENCILS
JONATHAN GLAPION INKS
GURU eFX'S HARTMAN and BEVARD COLORS
NORTON, GLAPION and GURU COVER
DAVE SHARPE LETTERER
TOM VALENTE PRODUCTION
NATHAN COSBY ASST. EDITOR
MACKENZIE CADENHEAD EDITOR
MARK PANICCIA CONSULTING EDITOR
JOE QUESADA CHIEF
DAN BUCKLEY PUBLISHER

MARVEL
Spotlight

VISIT US AT
www.abdopublishing.com

Spotlight library bound edition © 2007. Spotlight is a division of ABDO Publishing Company, Edina, Minnesota.

Cataloging Data

McKeever, Sean
   Make mine Mysterio! / Sean McKeever, writer ; Mike Norton, pencils ; Jonathan Glapion, inks -- Library bound ed.
      p. cm. -- (Spider-Man)
   Summary: Introduces readers of all ages to some of the greatest stories of the legendary Marvel Universe.
   "Marvel age"--Cover..
   Revision of the February 2006 issue of Marvel adventures Spider-Man.
   ISBN-13: 978-1-59961-211-9 (Reinforced Library Bound Edition)
   ISBN-10: 1-59961-211-9 (Reinforced Library Bound Edition)
      1. Spider-Man (Fictitious character)--Fiction. 2. Comic books, strips, etc.--Fiction. 3. Graphic novels. I. Title. II. Series.

741.5dc22

All Spotlight books are reinforced library binding
and manufactured in the United States of America

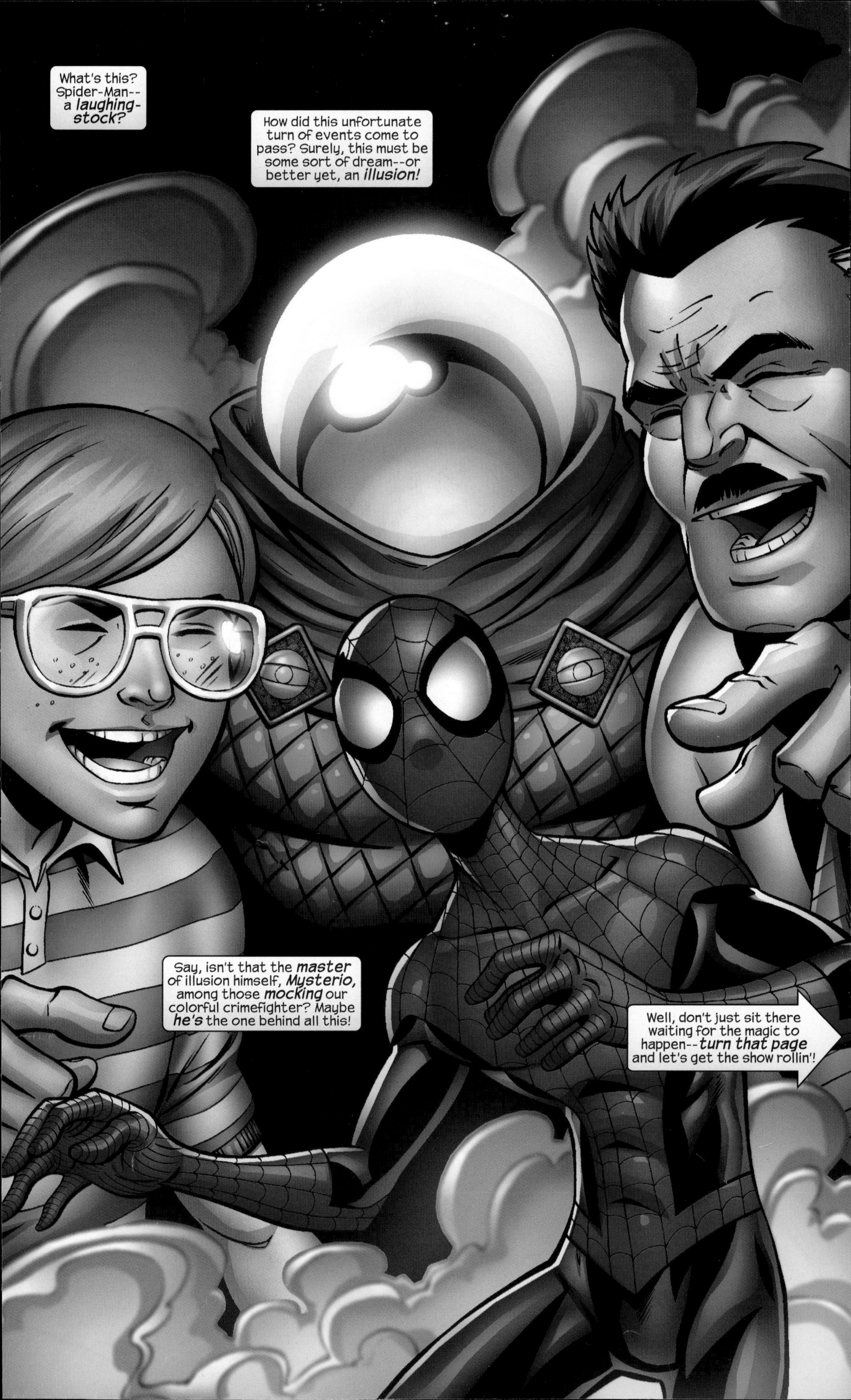
What's this? Spider-Man-- a *laughing-stock?*
How did this unfortunate turn of events come to pass? Surely, this must be some sort of dream--or better yet, an *illusion!*
Say, isn't that the *master* of illusion himself, *Mysterio,* among those *mocking* our colorful crimefighter? Maybe *he's* the one behind all this!
Well, don't just sit there waiting for the magic to happen--*turn that page* and let's get the show rollin'!

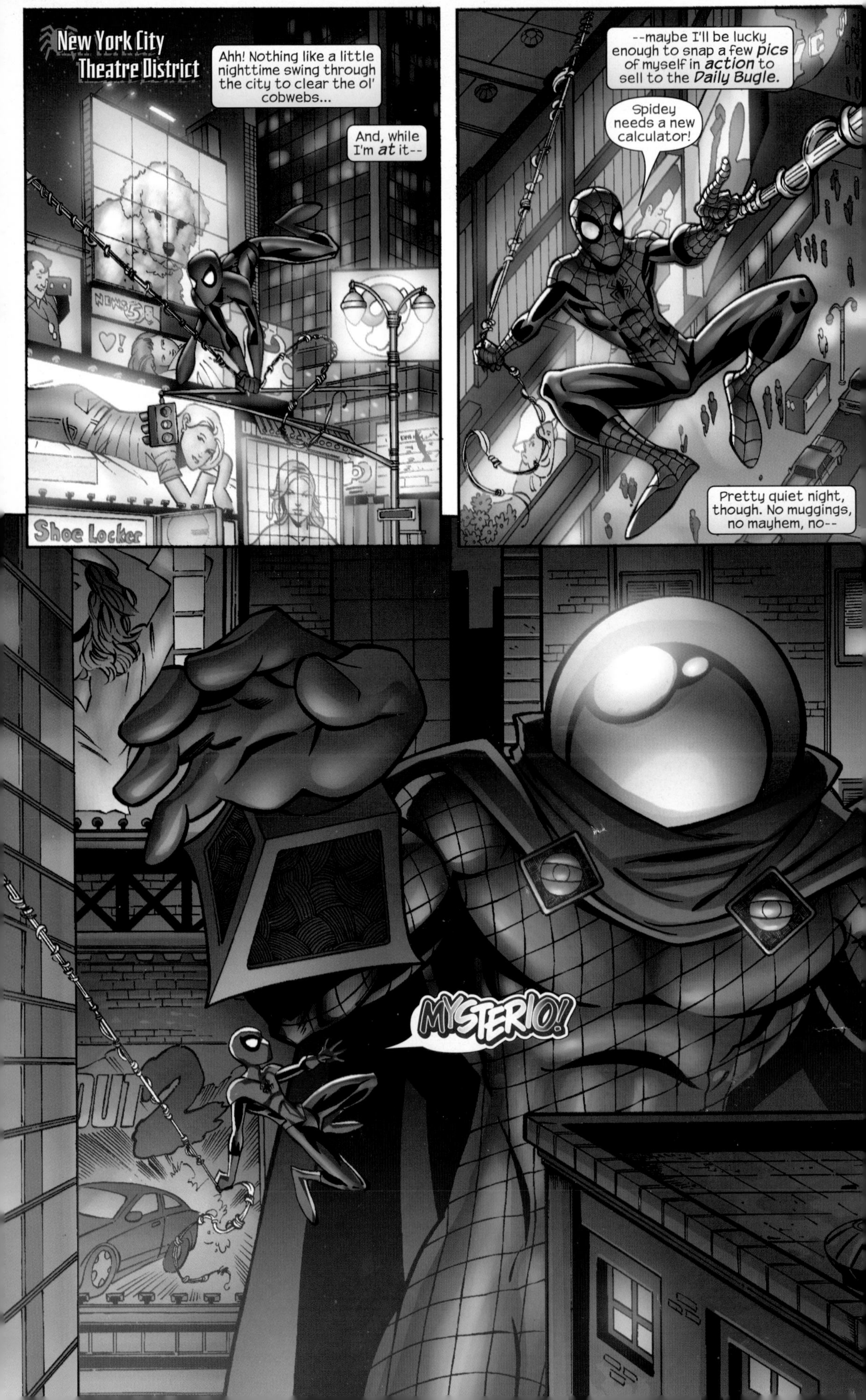
New York City
Theatre District
Ahh! Nothing like a little nighttime swing through the city to clear the ol' cobwebs...
And, while I'm *at* it--
--maybe I'll be lucky enough to snap a few *pics* of myself in *action* to sell to the *Daily Bugle*.
Spidey needs a new calculator!
Pretty quiet night, though. No muggings, no mayhem, no--
MYSTERIO!
Shoe Locker

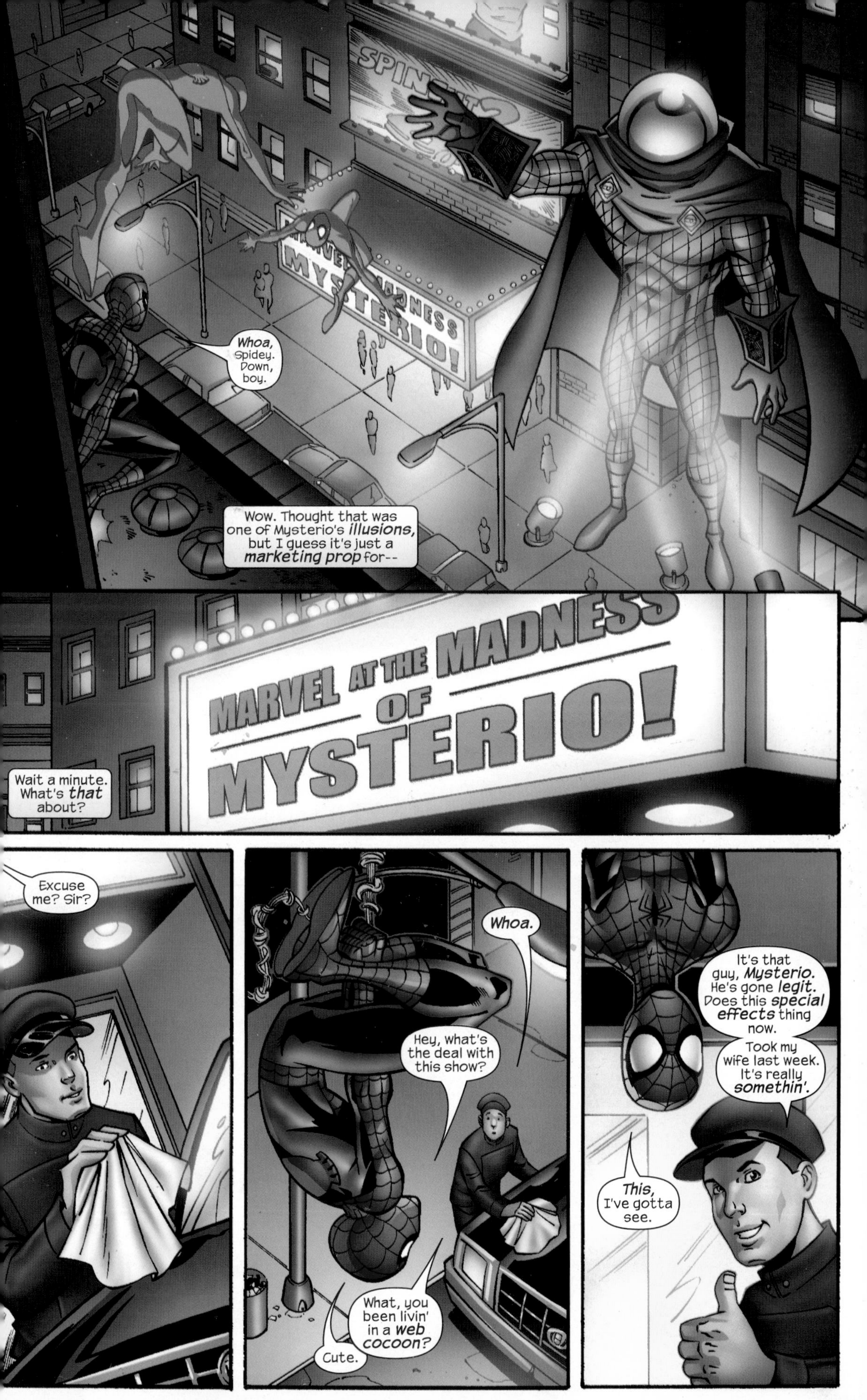

SPINSATIONS
MARVEL AT THE MADNESS OF MYSTERIO!
Whoa, Spidey. Down, boy.
Wow. Thought that was one of Mysterio's illusions, but I guess it's just a marketing prop for--
MARVEL AT THE MADNESS OF MYSTERIO!
Wait a minute. What's that about?
Excuse me? Sir?
Whoa.
Hey, what's the deal with this show?
What, you been livin' in a web cocoon?
Cute.
It's that guy, Mysterio. He's gone legit. Does this special effects thing now.
Took my wife last week. It's really somethin'.
This, I've gotta see.

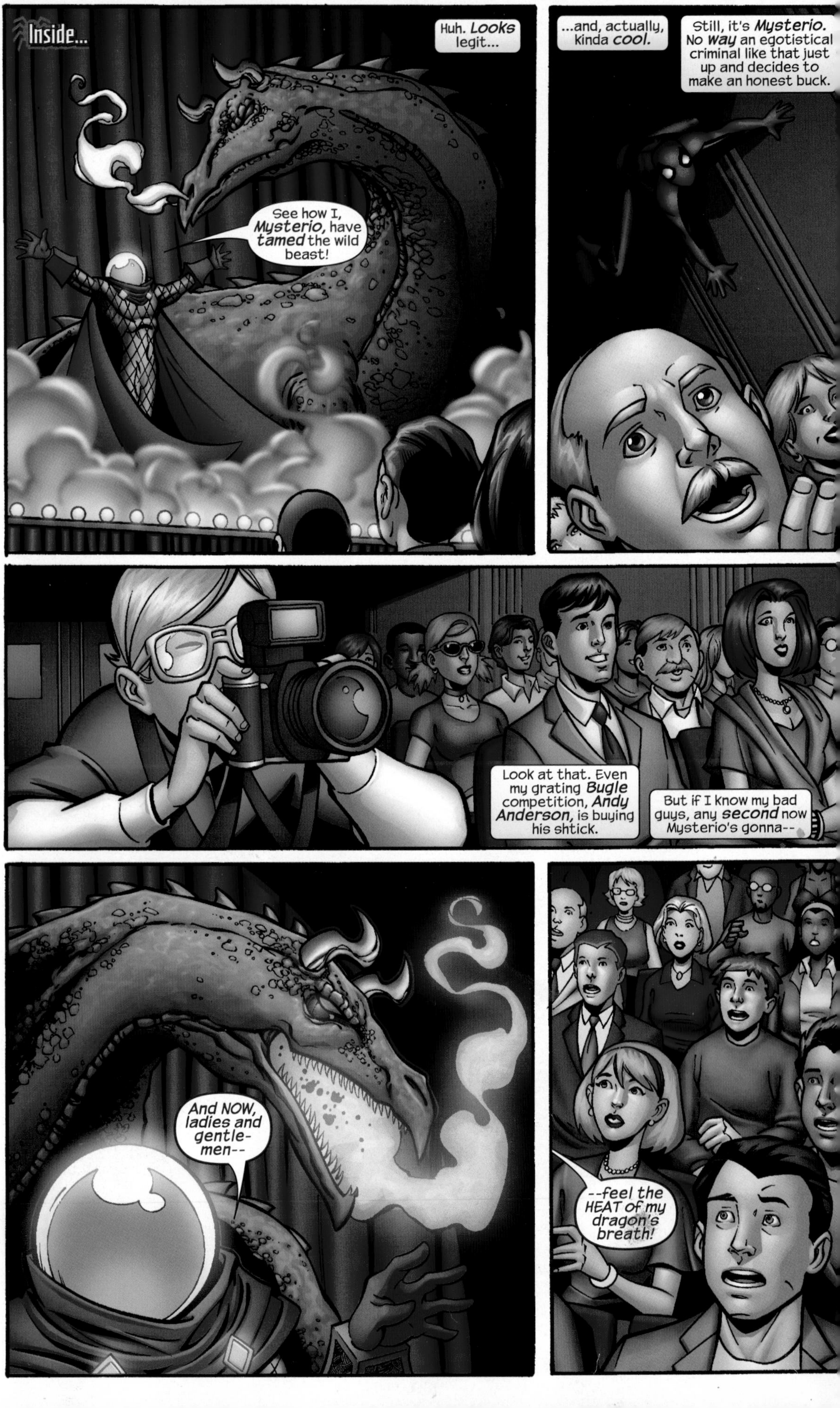
Inside...
Huh. Looks legit...
See how I, Mysterio, have tamed the wild beast!
...and, actually, kinda cool.
Still, it's Mysterio. No way an egotistical criminal like that just up and decides to make an honest buck.
Look at that. Even my grating Bugle competition, Andy Anderson, is buying his shtick.
But if I know my bad guys, any second now Mysterio's gonna--
And NOW, ladies and gentle- men--
--feel the HEAT of my dragon's breath!

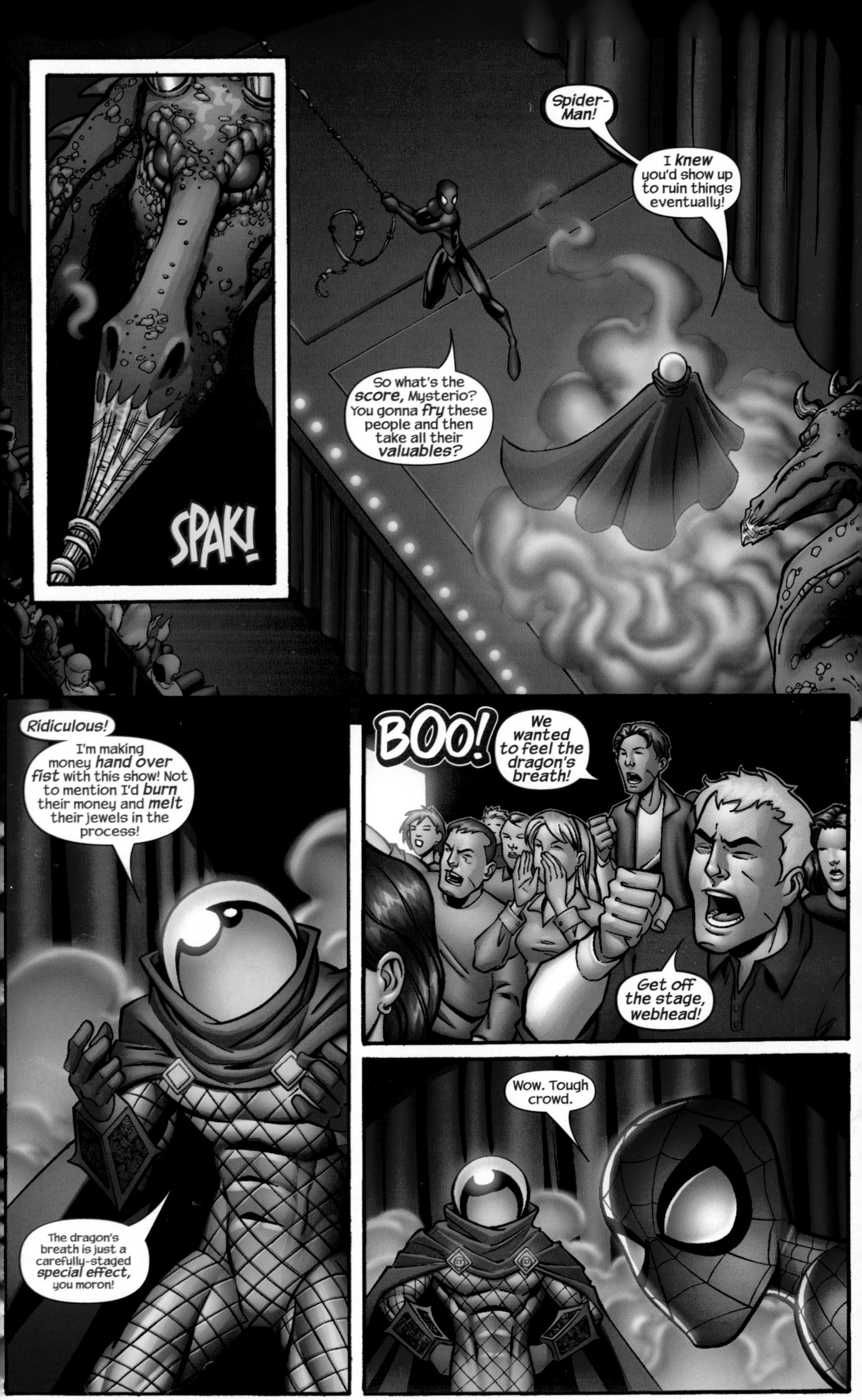
SPAK!
Spider-Man!
I knew you'd show up to ruin things eventually!
So what's the score, Mysterio? You gonna fry these people and then take all their valuables?
Ridiculous!
I'm making money hand over fist with this show! Not to mention I'd burn their money and melt their jewels in the process!
The dragon's breath is just a carefully-staged special effect, you moron!
BOO!
We wanted to feel the dragon's breath!
Get off the stage, webhead!
Wow. Tough crowd.

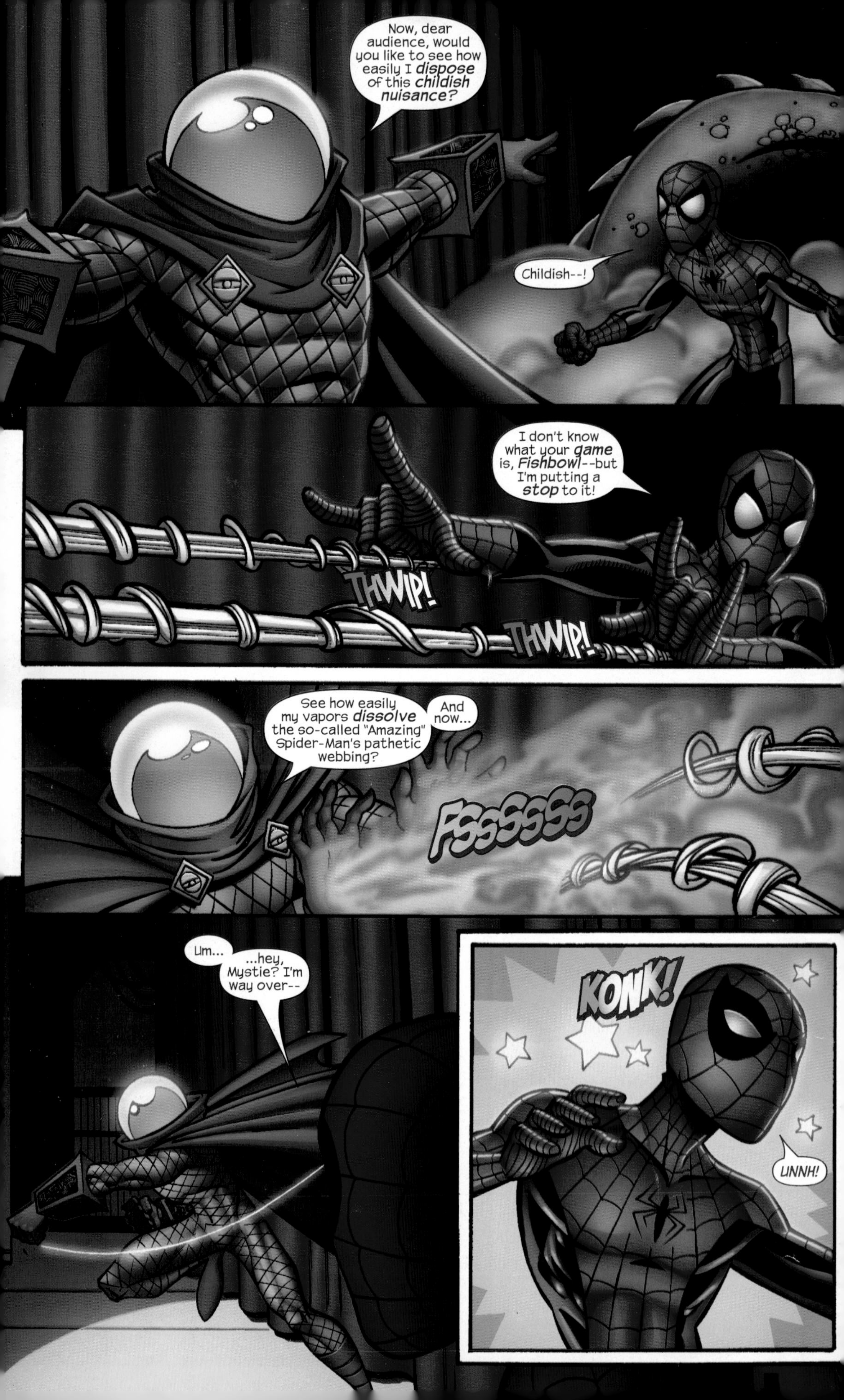

Now, dear audience, would you like to see how easily I dispose of this childish nuisance?
Childish--!
I don't know what your game is, Fishbowl--but I'm putting a stop to it!
THWIP!
THWIP!
See how easily my vapors dissolve the so-called "Amazing" Spider-Man's pathetic webbing?
And now...
FSSSSSS
Um...
...hey, Mystie? I'm way over--
KONK!
UNNH!

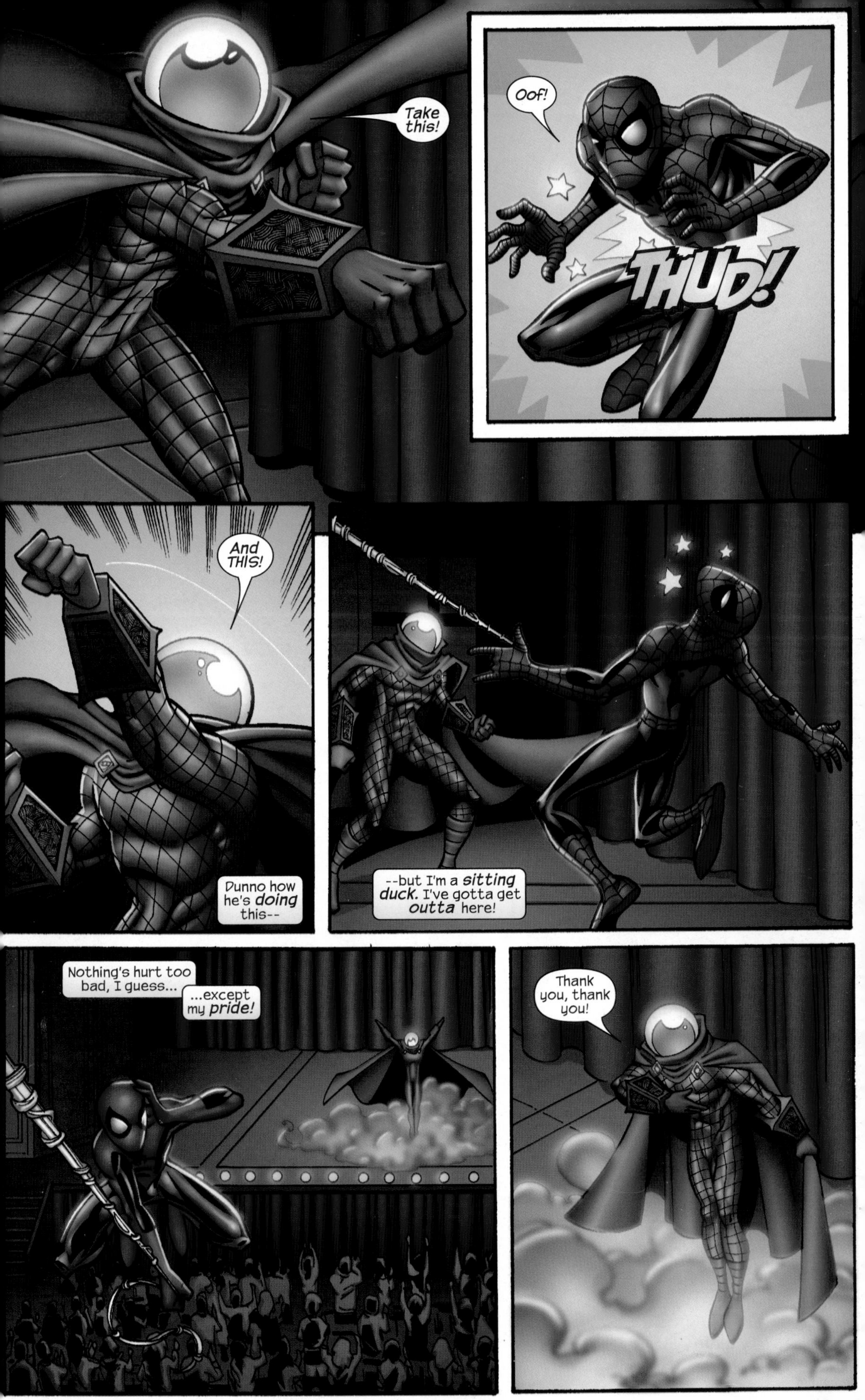
Take this!
Oof!
THUD!
And THIS!
Dunno how he's doing this--
--but I'm a sitting duck. I've gotta get outta here!
Nothing's hurt too bad, I guess...
...except my pride!
Thank you, thank you!

See *that*, Parker? Finally, that menace *Spider-Man* gets what he deserves!

DAILY BUGLE

SPIDER-MAN SLAMMED BY MYSTERIO!

Meets Humiliating Defeat, Flees Before Live Audience

PHOTO BY A. ANDERSON

City. Last night a showdown took place between the menace Spider-Man and the seemingly legit... the two have been known to throw dow... e of a bridge, endangering inn... sterio is performing his... e in the heart of...

Remind me to send *Mysterio* my *warmest* regards! Maybe even a five-dollar coupon toward a *Bugle* subscription...

You're a *prince*, Mr. Jameson.

Greetings and *salutations*, fellow photog!

Oh no...

Here's the little go-getter who made today's paper *sing!* You could *learn* a thing or two from this kid, Parker!

Now *scoot*, you two! I'm a busy man!

Go talk about your *bubblegum cards* and *gaming cartridges!*

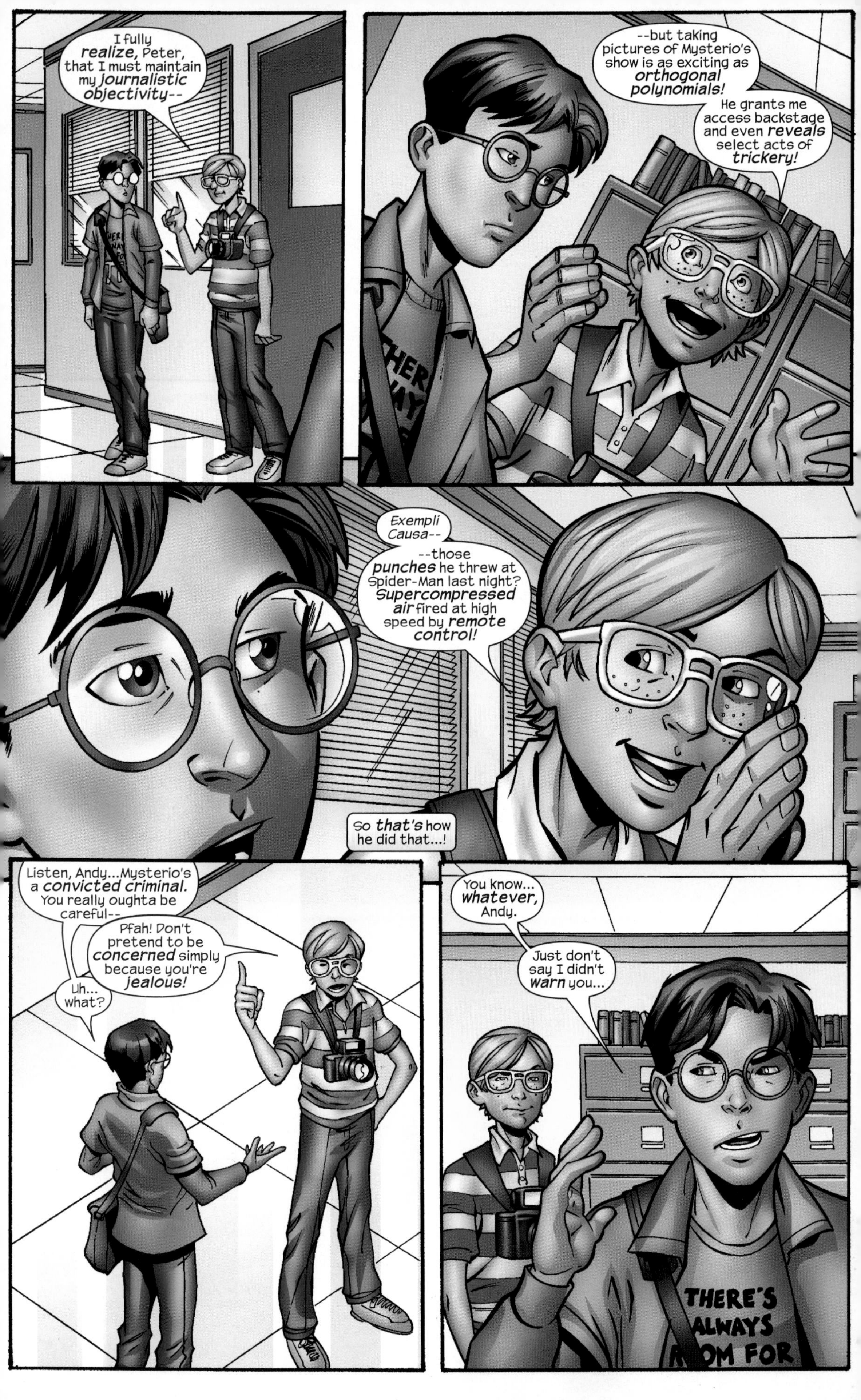
I fully realize, Peter, that I must maintain my journalistic objectivity--
--but taking pictures of Mysterio's show is as exciting as orthogonal polynomials!
He grants me access backstage and even reveals select acts of trickery!
Exempli Causa--
--those punches he threw at Spider-Man last night? Supercompressed air fired at high speed by remote control!
So that's how he did that...!
Listen, Andy...Mysterio's a convicted criminal. You really oughta be careful--
Pfah! Don't pretend to be concerned simply because you're jealous!
Uh... what?
You know... whatever, Andy.
Just don't say I didn't warn you...
THERE'S ALWAYS ROOM FOR

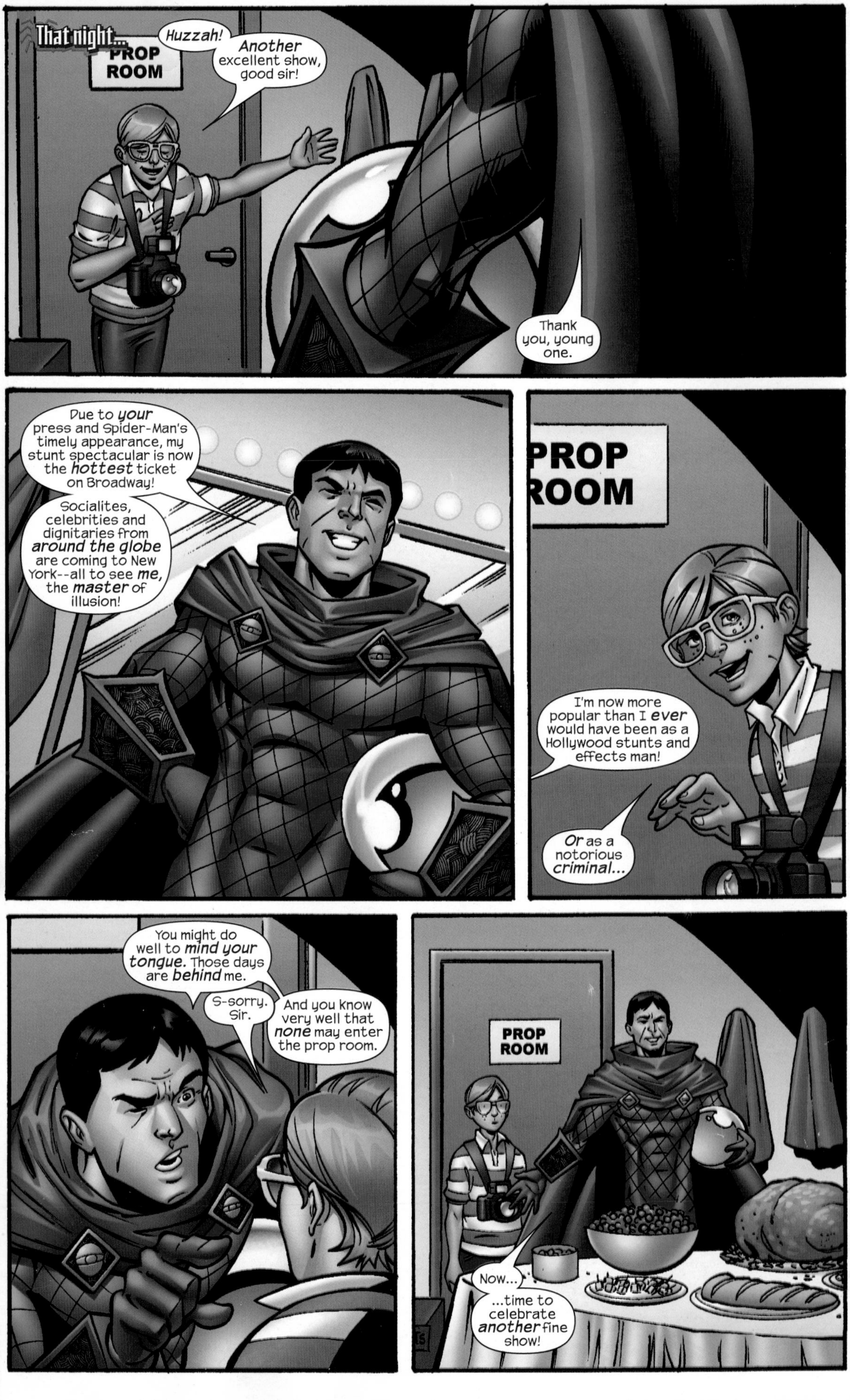
That night...
PROP ROOM
Huzzah!
Another excellent show, good sir!
Thank you, young one.
Due to your press and Spider-Man's timely appearance, my stunt spectacular is now the hottest ticket on Broadway!
Socialites, celebrities and dignitaries from around the globe are coming to New York--all to see me, the master of illusion!
PROP ROOM
I'm now more popular than I ever would have been as a Hollywood stunts and effects man!
Or as a notorious criminal...
You might do well to mind your tongue. Those days are behind me.
S-sorry. Sir.
And you know very well that none may enter the prop room.
PROP ROOM
Now...
...time to celebrate another fine show!

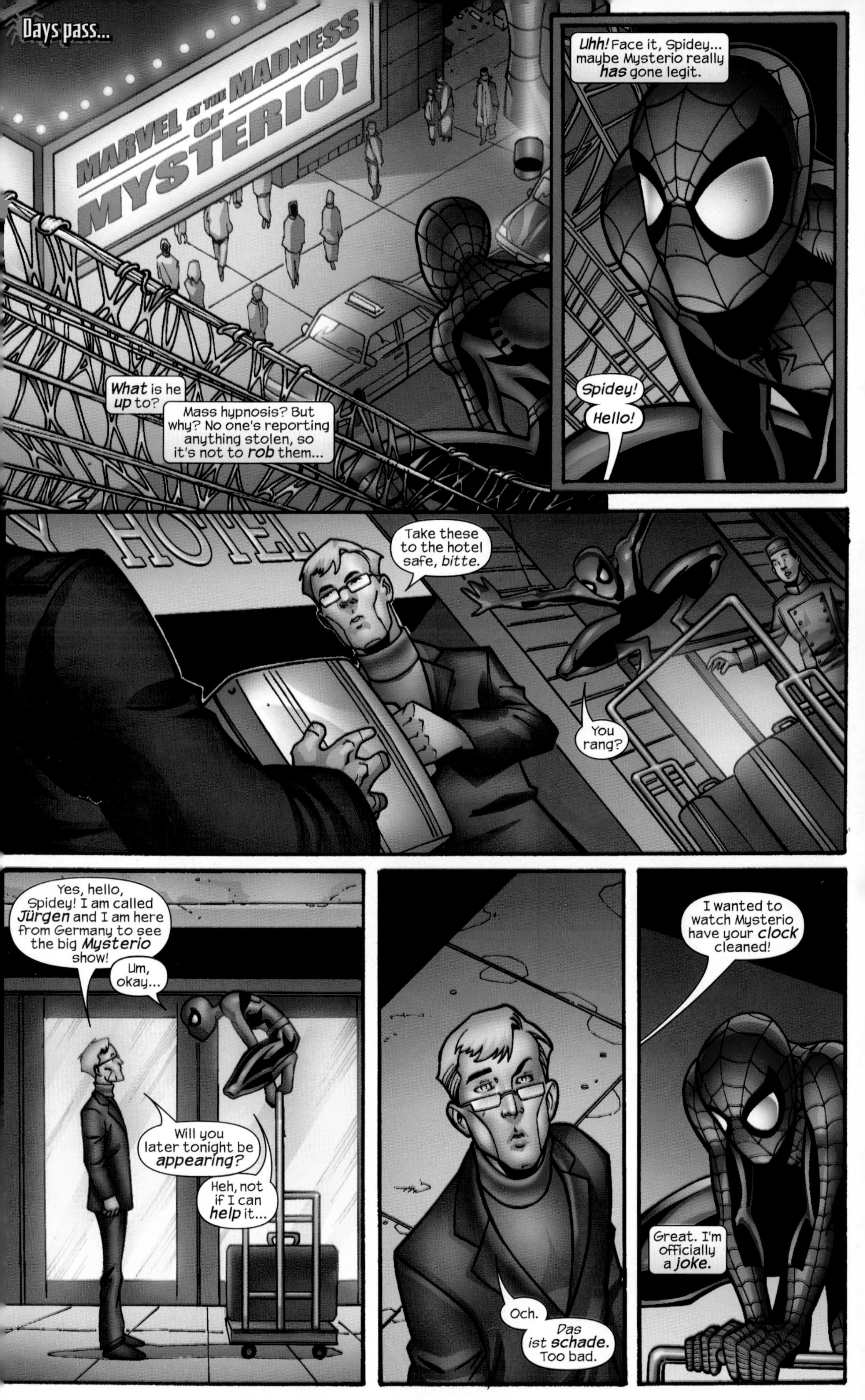
Days pass...
MARVEL AT THE MADNESS OF MYSTERIO!
What is he up to?
Mass hypnosis? But why? No one's reporting anything stolen, so it's not to rob them...
Uhh! Face it, Spidey... maybe Mysterio really has gone legit.
Spidey!
Hello!
HOTEL
Take these to the hotel safe, bitte.
You rang?
Yes, hello, Spidey! I am called Jürgen and I am here from Germany to see the big Mysterio show!
Um, okay...
Will you later tonight be appearing?
Heh, not if I can help it...
Och.
Das ist schade. Too bad.
I wanted to watch Mysterio have your clock cleaned!
Great. I'm officially a joke.

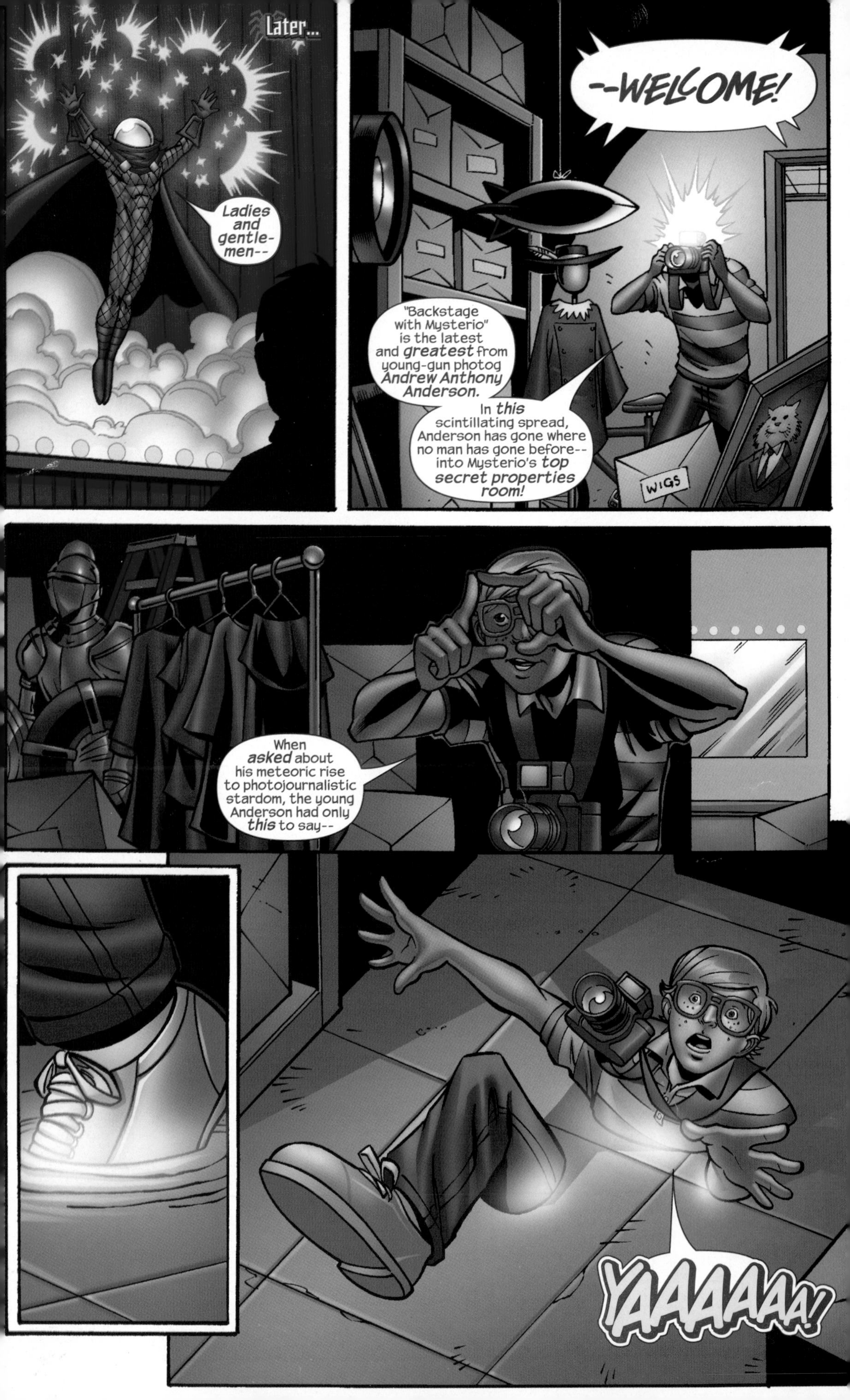
Later...
Ladies and gentle-men--
--WELCOME!
"Backstage with Mysterio" is the latest and greatest from young-gun photog Andrew Anthony Anderson.
In this scintillating spread, Anderson has gone where no man has gone before--into Mysterio's top secret properties room!
WIGS
When asked about his meteoric rise to photojournalistic stardom, the young Anderson had only this to say--
YAAAAAA!

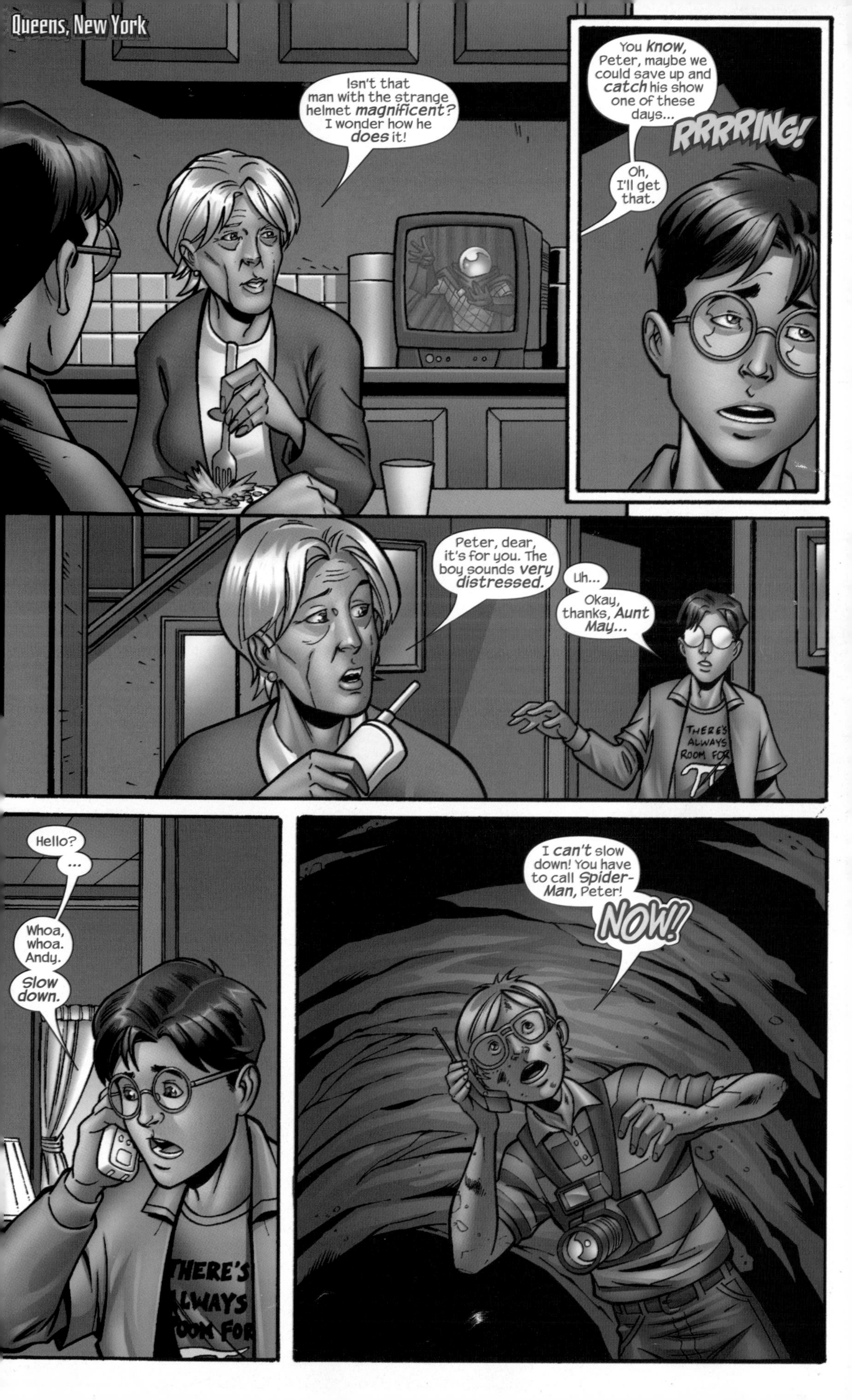
Queens, New York
Isn't that man with the strange helmet magnificent? I wonder how he does it!
You know, Peter, maybe we could save up and catch his show one of these days...
RRRRING!
Oh, I'll get that.
Peter, dear, it's for you. The boy sounds very distressed.
Uh...
Okay, thanks, Aunt May...
THERE'S ALWAYS ROOM FOR
Hello?
...
Whoa, whoa. Andy.
Slow down.
I can't slow down! You have to call Spider-Man, Peter!
NOW!!
THERE'S ALWAYS ROOM FOR

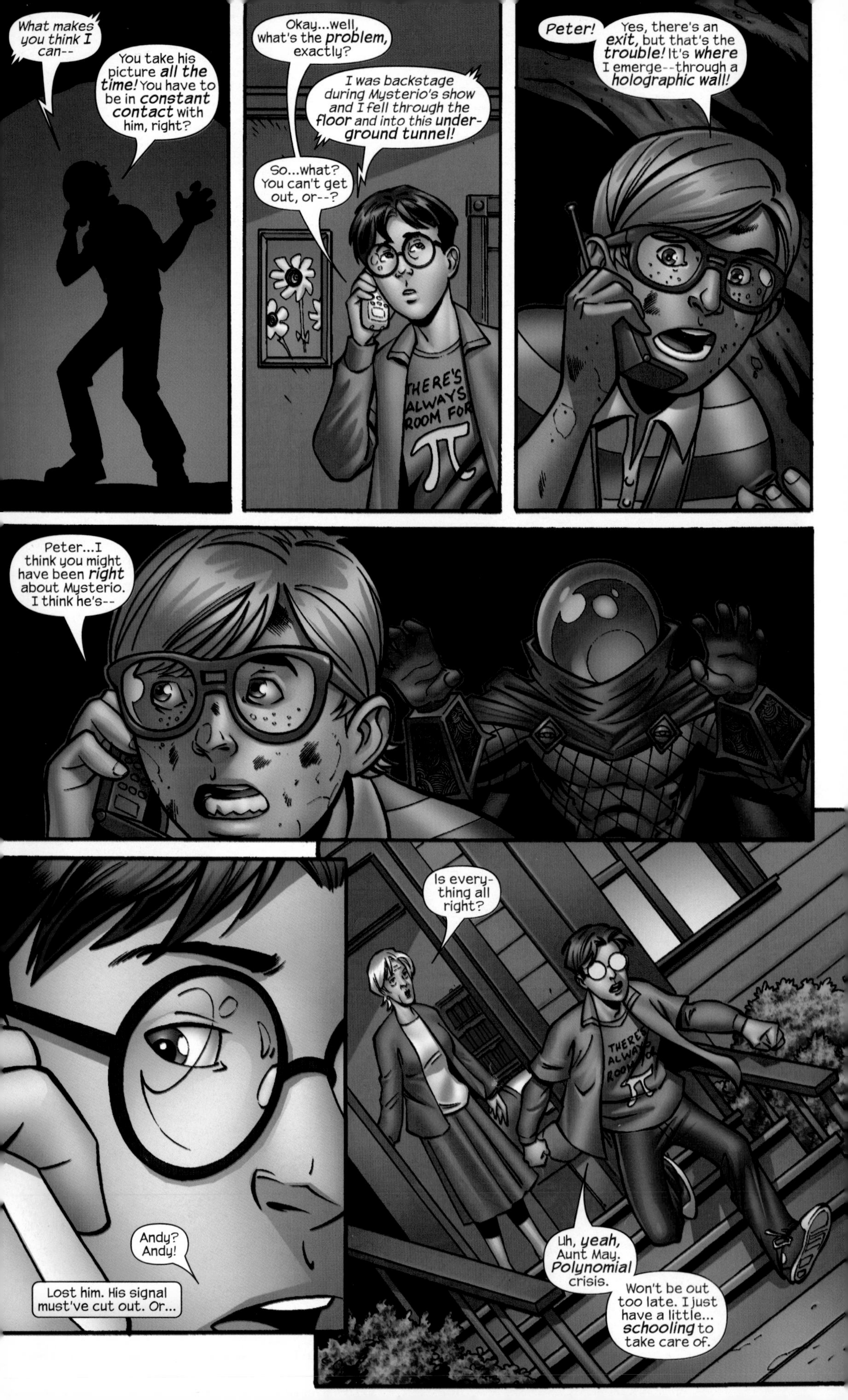
What makes you think I can--
You take his picture all the time! You have to be in constant contact with him, right?
Okay...well, what's the problem, exactly?
I was backstage during Mysterio's show and I fell through the floor and into this underground tunnel!
So...what? You can't get out, or--?
THERE'S ALWAYS ROOM FOR π
Peter!
Yes, there's an exit, but that's the trouble! It's where I emerge--through a holographic wall!
Peter...I think you might have been right about Mysterio. I think he's--
Andy? Andy!
Lost him. His signal must've cut out. Or...
Is everything all right?
Uh, yeah, Aunt May. Polynomial crisis.
Won't be out too late. I just have a little... schooling to take care of.

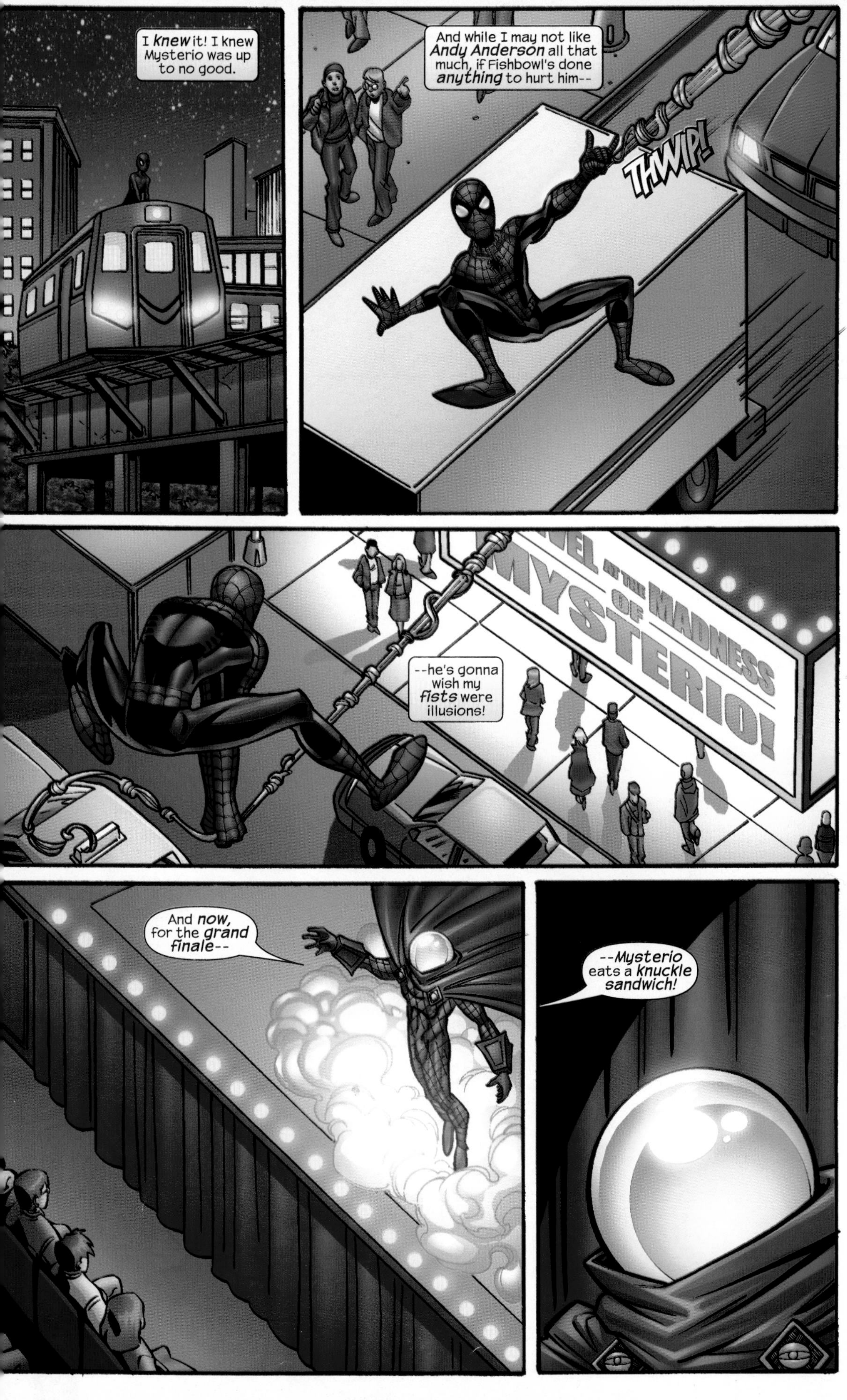
I knew it! I knew Mysterio was up to no good.
And while I may not like Andy Anderson all that much, if Fishbowl's done anything to hurt him--
THWIP!
MARVEL AT THE MADNESS OF MYSTERIO!
--he's gonna wish my fists were illusions!
And now, for the grand finale--
--Mysterio eats a knuckle sandwich!

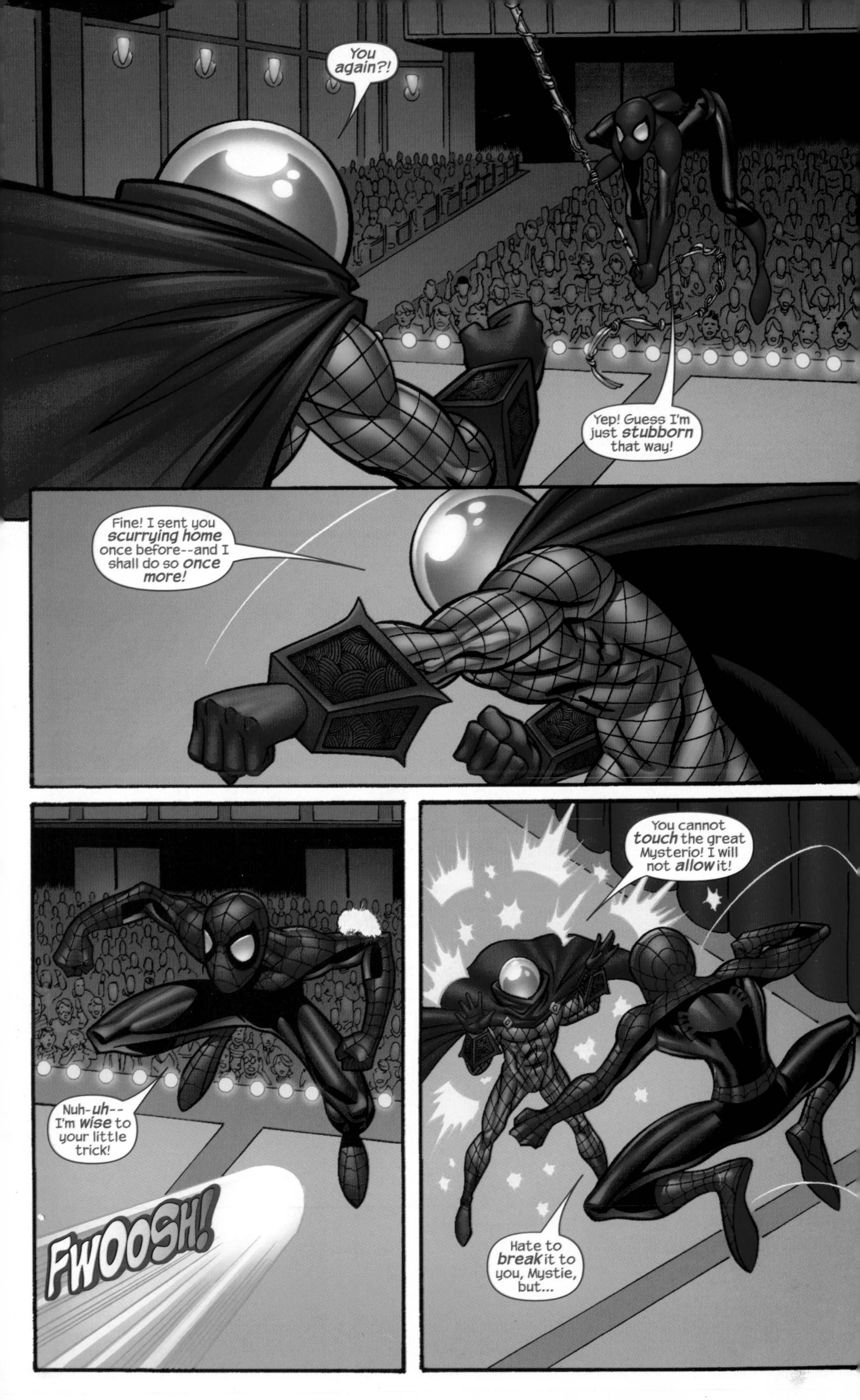
You again?!
Yep! Guess I'm just stubborn that way!
Fine! I sent you scurrying home once before--and I shall do so once more!
Nuh-uh-- I'm wise to your little trick!
FWOOSH!
You cannot touch the great Mysterio! I will not allow it!
Hate to break it to you, Mystie, but...

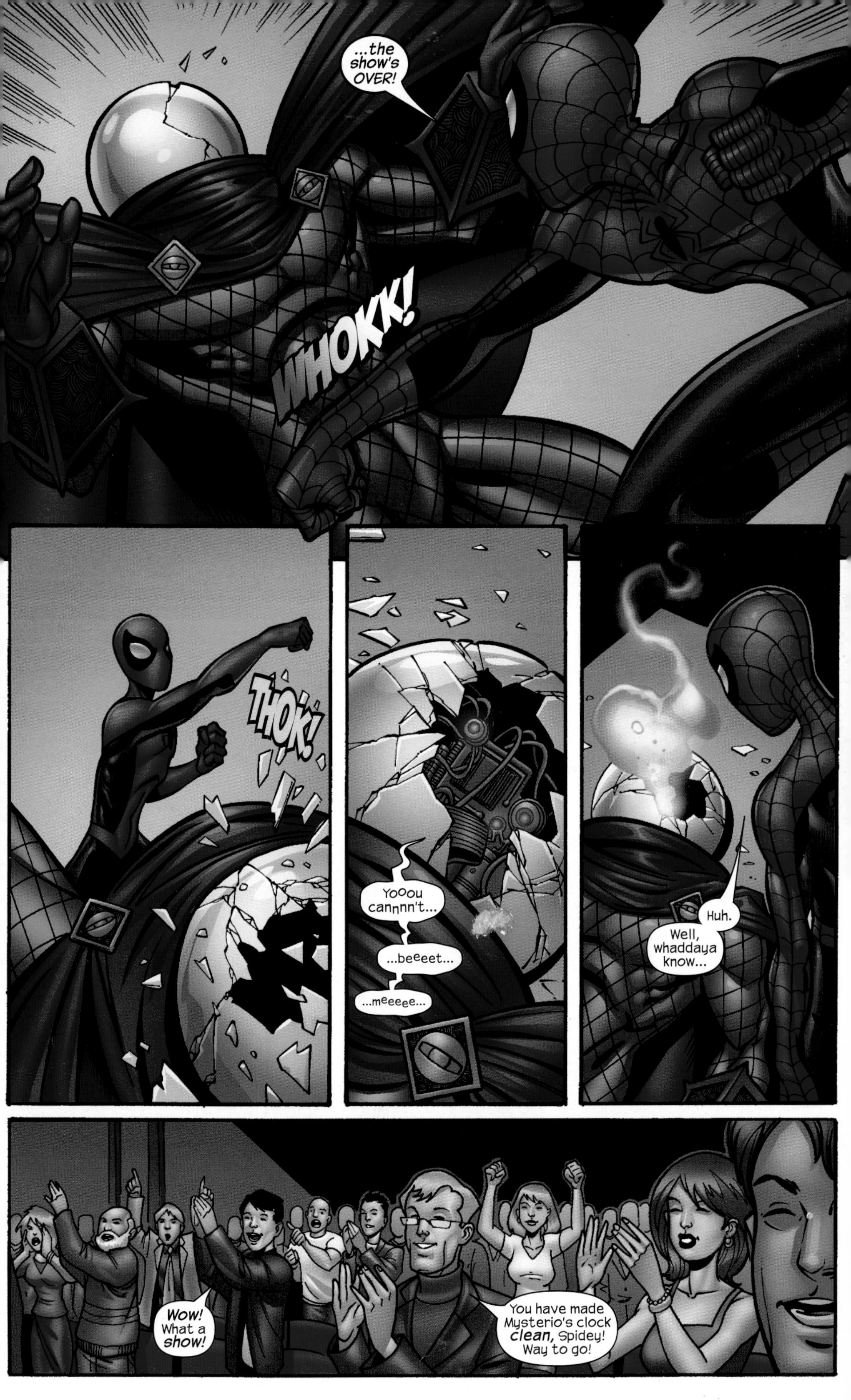
...the show's OVER!
WHOKK!
THOK!
Yooou cannnnn't...
...beeeet...
...meeeee...
Huh. Well, whaddaya know...
Wow! What a show!
You have made Mysterio's clock clean, Spidey! Way to go!

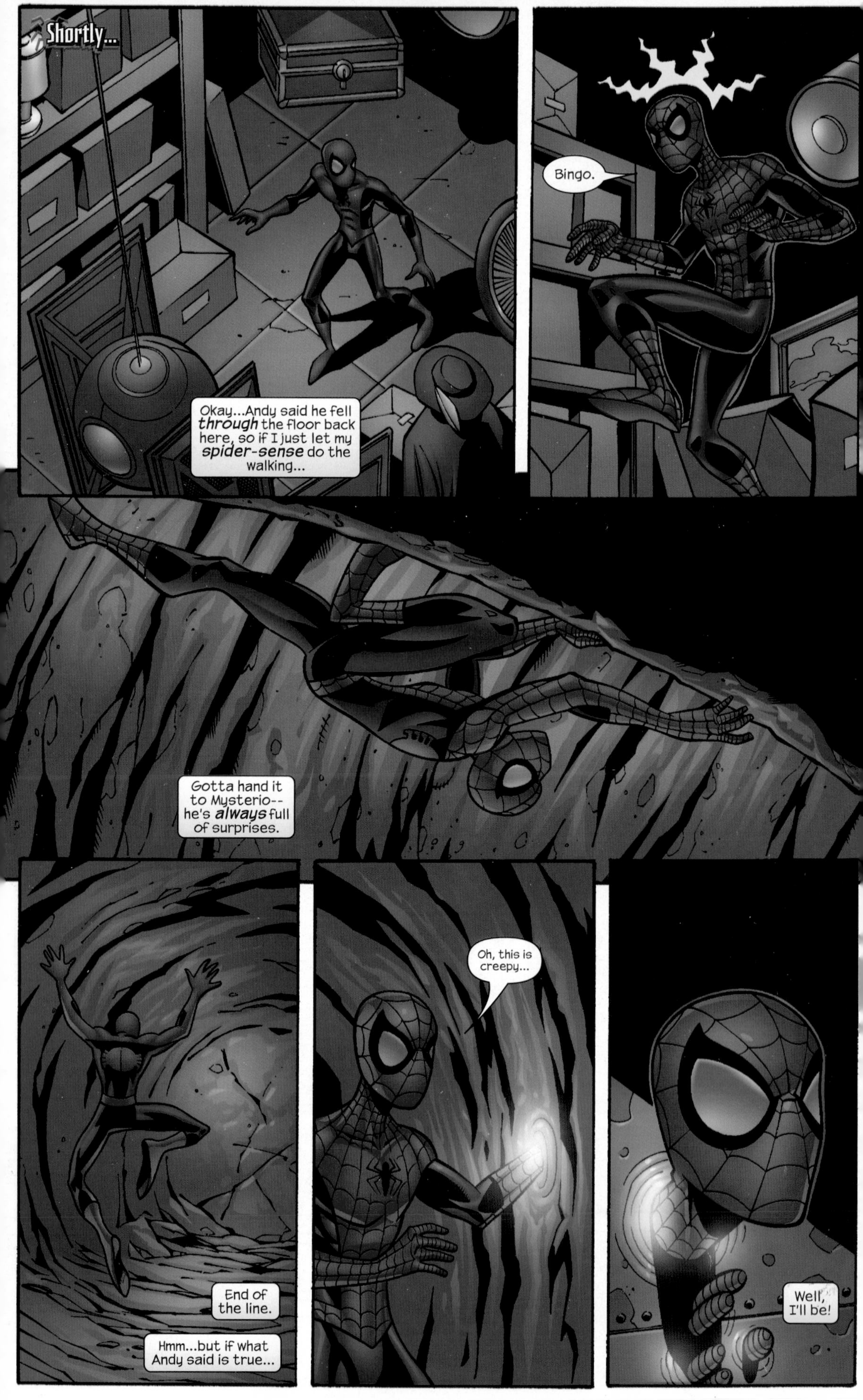
Shortly...
Okay...Andy said he fell through the floor back here, so if I just let my spider-sense do the walking...
Bingo.
Gotta hand it to Mysterio--he's always full of surprises.
End of the line.
Hmm...but if what Andy said is true...
Oh, this is creepy...
Well, I'll be!

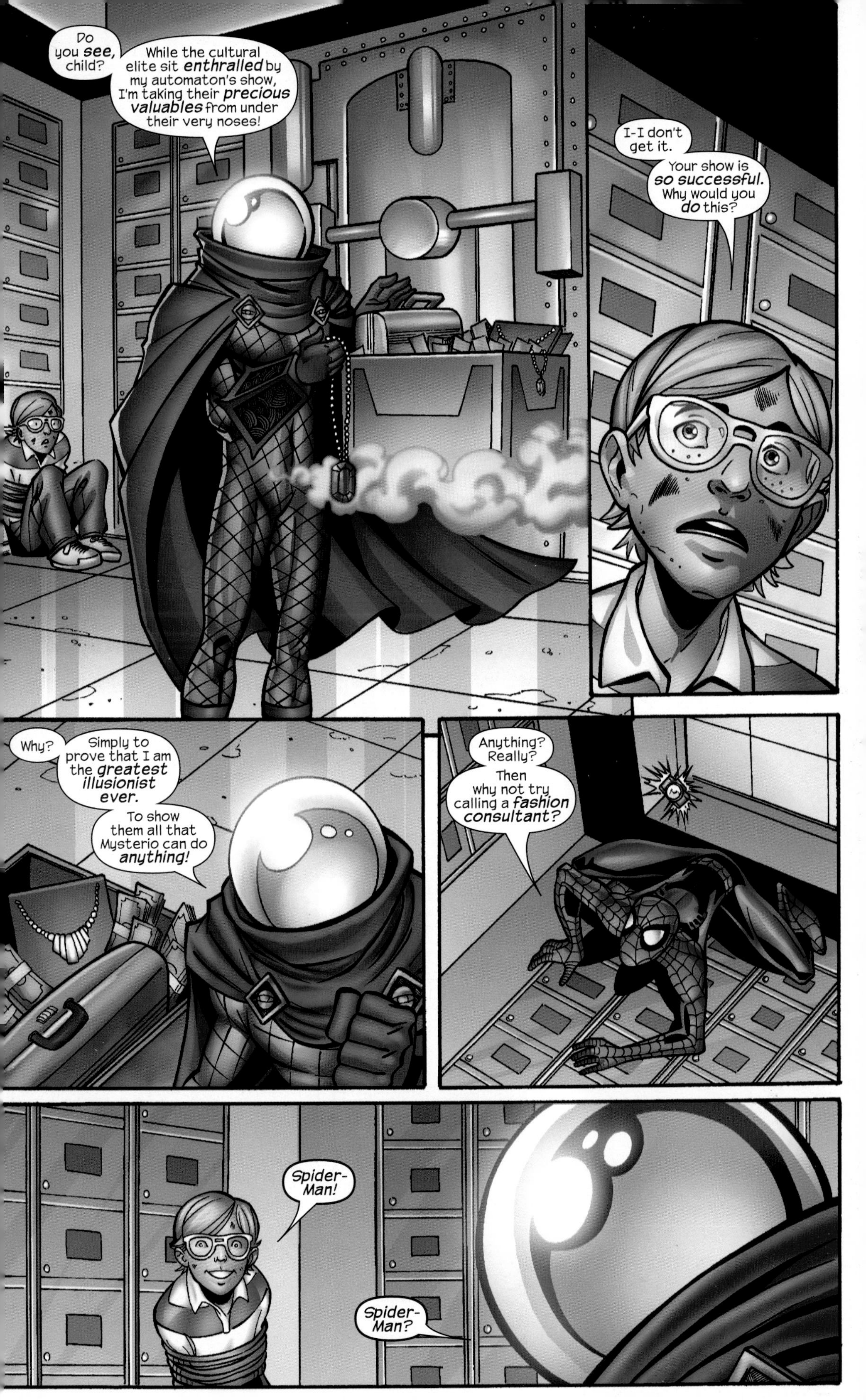

Do you see, child?
While the cultural elite sit enthralled by my automaton's show, I'm taking their precious valuables from under their very noses!
I-I don't get it.
Your show is so successful. Why would you do this?
Why?
Simply to prove that I am the greatest illusionist ever.
To show them all that Mysterio can do anything!
Anything? Really?
Then why not try calling a fashion consultant?
Spider-Man!
Spider-Man?

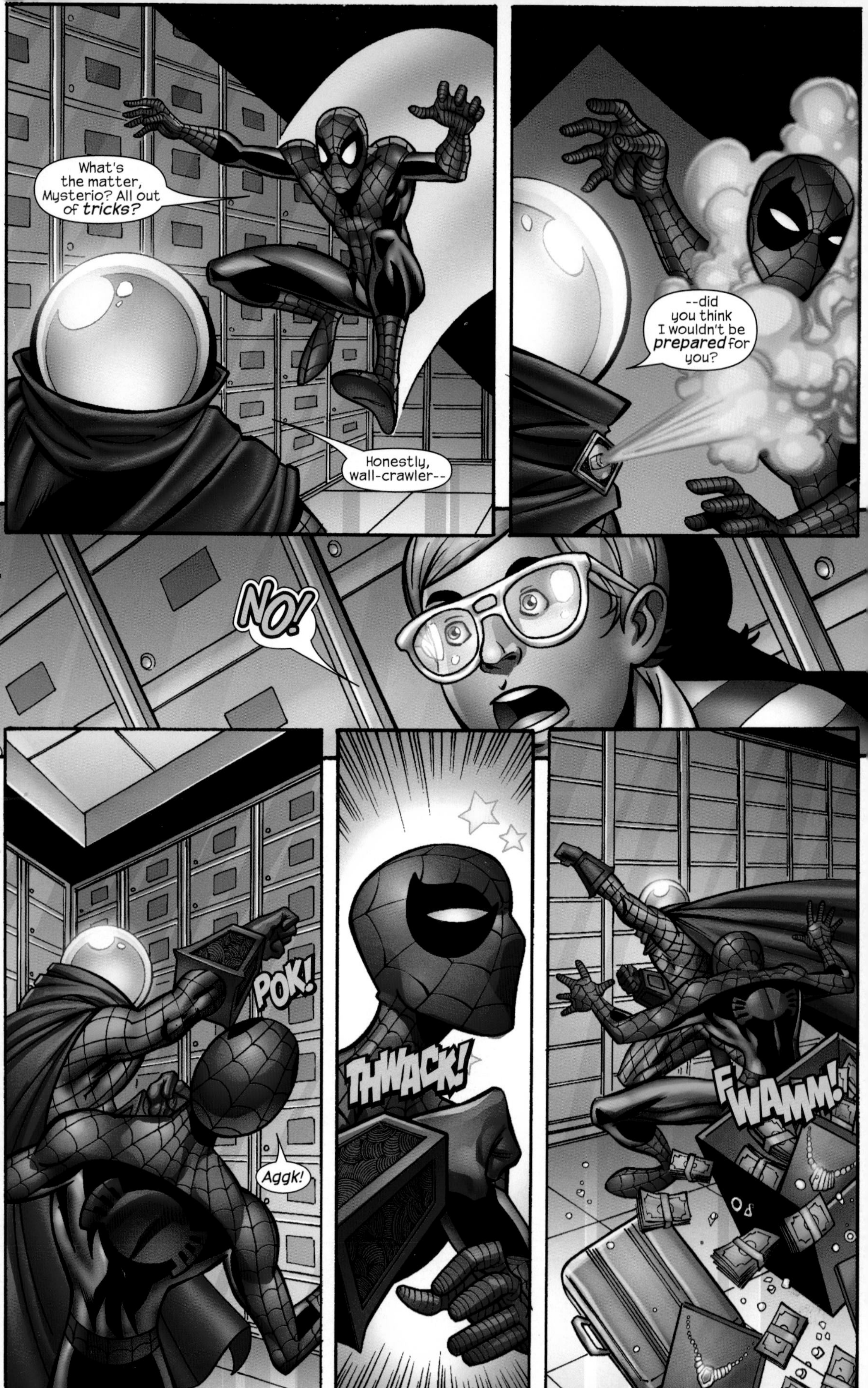
What's the matter, Mysterio? All out of *tricks?*
Honestly, wall-crawler--
--did you think I wouldn't be *prepared* for you?
NO!
POK!
Aggk!
THWACK!
FWAMM!

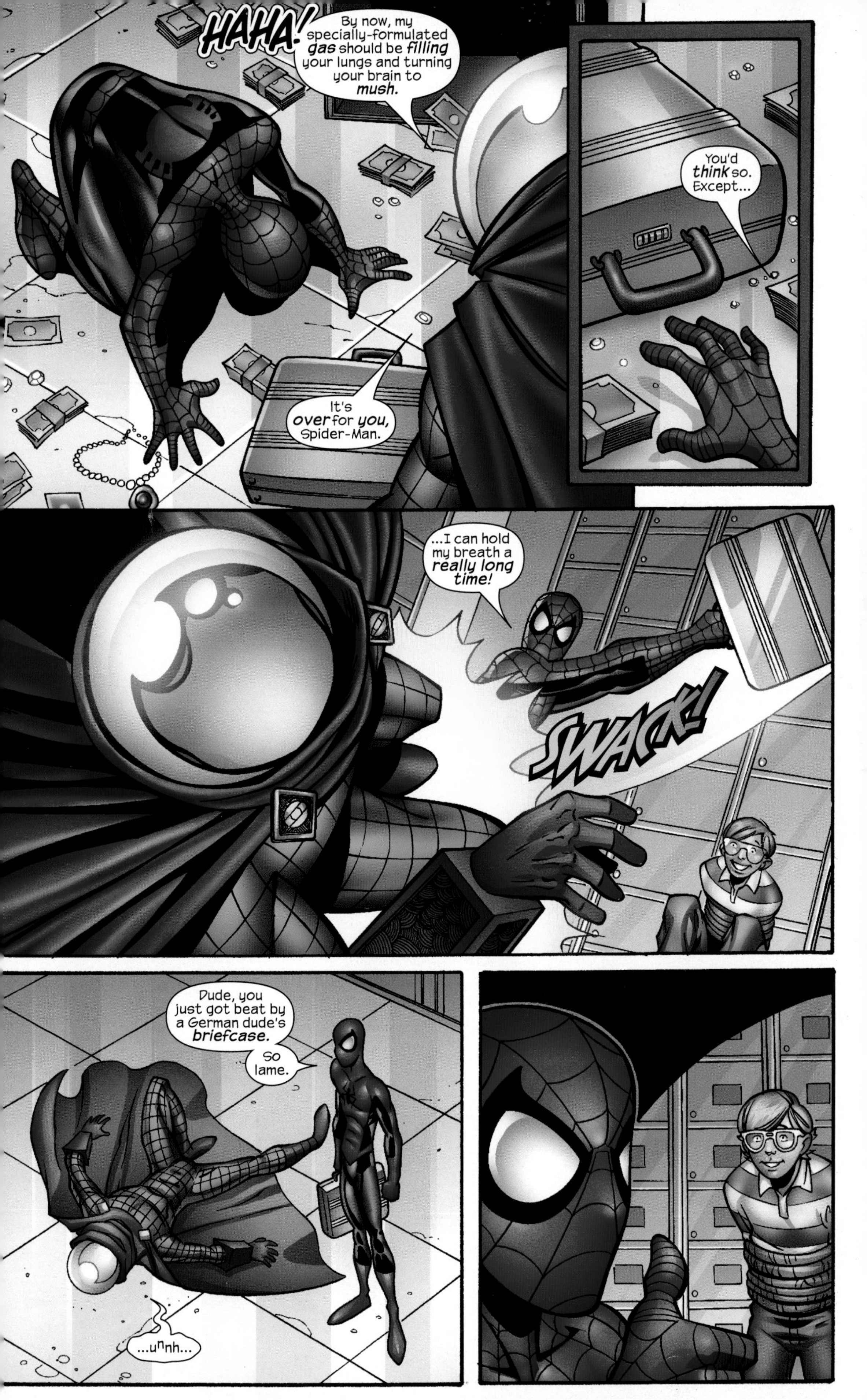

HAHA!
By now, my specially-formulated gas should be filling your lungs and turning your brain to mush.
It's over for you, Spider-Man.
You'd think so. Except...
...I can hold my breath a really long time!
SWACK!
Dude, you just got beat by a German dude's briefcase.
So lame.
...unnh...

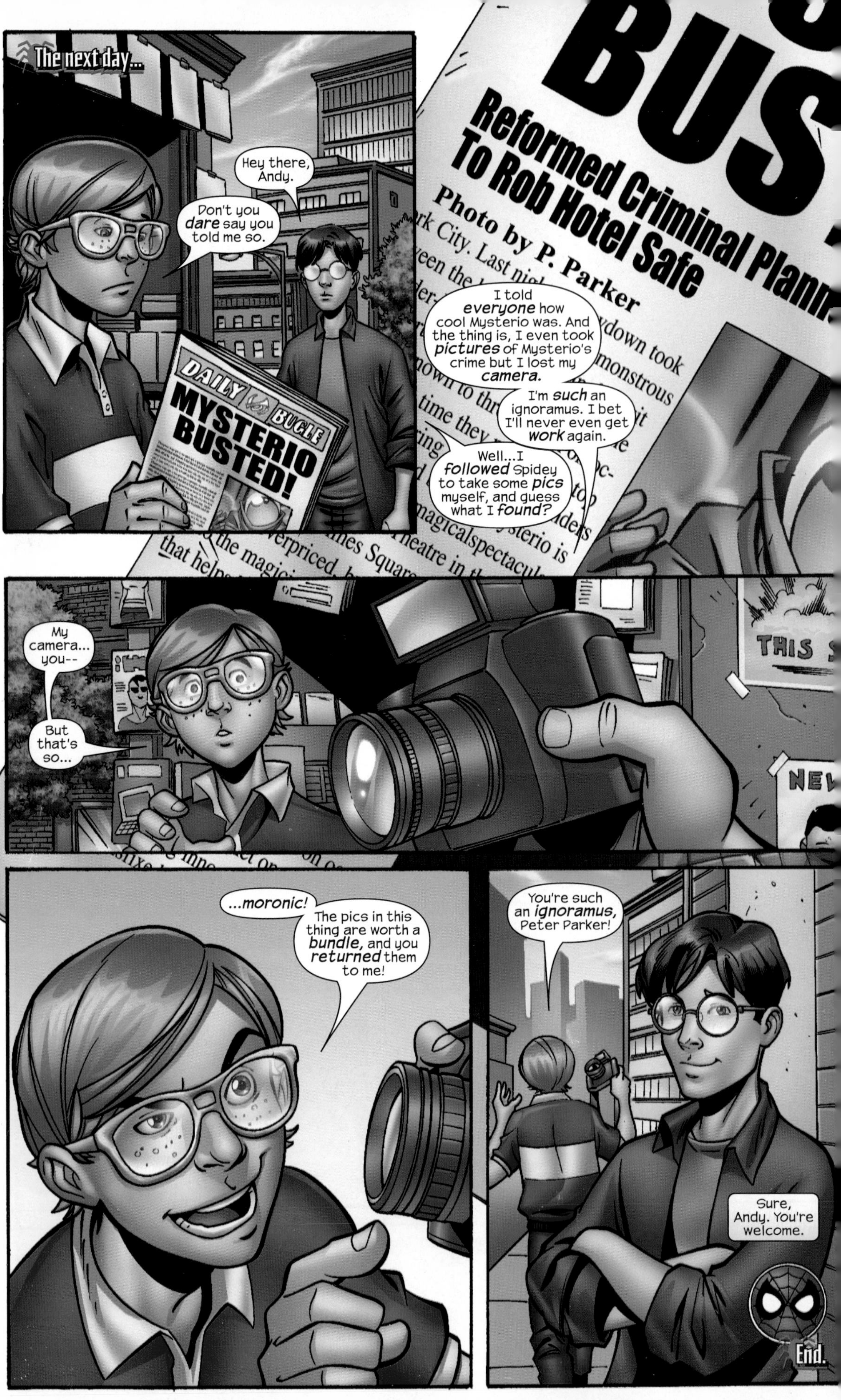

The next day...
Hey there, Andy.
Don't you dare say you told me so.
DAILY BUGLE
MYSTERIO BUSTED!
To Rob Hotel Safe
Photo by P. Parker
I told everyone how cool Mysterio was. And the thing is, I even took pictures of Mysterio's crime but I lost my camera.
I'm such an ignoramus. I bet I'll never even get work again.
Well...I followed Spidey to take some pics myself, and guess what I found?
My camera... you--
But that's so...
THIS
...moronic!
The pics in this thing are worth a bundle, and you returned them to me!
You're such an ignoramus, Peter Parker!
Sure, Andy. You're welcome.
End.